Book 1
The Man in the Mist

Reading Practice

Words at CVC and CVCC level

(C = consonant, V = vowel)

cub	and
gap	end
jog	ant
win	imp
box	act
yet	cost
mess	bunk
fizz	pelt
puff	ramp
hill	milk

Contents

Vocabulary:

kid — a young goat

kin — a person's family

nag — old horse

dim — faintly lit, difficult to see

odd — strange

Chapter 1
"Get Up!"

Zak is in bed. His pet kid is on the bed. The sun is up.

"Get off the bed! Get off the bed, Kid!" Zak sits up.

"Grandpa, get up!" Grandpa is not well. Grandpa cannot sit up.

Chapter 2
Zak Sets Off

Zak is sad. Grandpa is not well. Grandpa is his kin.

"I will get help. I will get the wagon. I can fix it to the nag."

Zak and the kid set off in the dim fog. It is cold and wet.

Chapter 3
The Man in the Mist

A man! A man in the fog!
Will the man rob him?

"Can I get on the wagon?" the man asks. The man has a big, red hat.

Zak and the man set off. The man is odd. The man has a box on his lap.

Chapter 4
The Odd Man

The man has a belt. It is a big belt. It is odd.

A pet rat is in the box.
The man hums and pats his rat.

The wagon jogs on. Is the man bad? Can Zak get rid of him?